# HEAVEN'S NOTE

KAYLA JARPPI

PUBLISHED BY

SIGMA'S
BOOKSHELF

MINNETONKA, MN 55305
WWW.SIGMASBOOKSHELF.COM

*Dedicated to the ones who have helped me and motivated me to continue on, even through life's many struggles: Danika, Jenna Lund, Tyla Pederson, Taylor Aschenbrenner, Natalie Schutz, the best school counselor, all of my teachers, and my photographer and friend Jillian Ulrich.*

# Foreword

Heaven's Note is a heart rending book hitting so many cords in the world of mental health challenges. Mental health is our personal well being and how that looks emotionally, psychologically, and socially. A person's mental health affects how he/she thinks, acts, and feels. Many factors, such as biological, life experiences, and family history, can contribute to a person's mental well being. All of these factors present themselves within Heaven's Note.

The author of Heaven's Note has a first hand understanding revolving around the challenges of mental health. While I don't have a full scope of all her factors, her mental health is certainly affected by her life experiences and family's history. The heart that is felt in this book is coming from a place of real fears and anxiety, but also genuine perseverance and resilience. The author digs deep to focus on the ugliest areas of mental health challenges some of our youth must endure due to the unchosen life experiences that are forced upon them. The author continues to struggle with her real challenges, but does so in a way that shows she wants to continue to persevere and be resilient.

The challenges the author's characters face are filled with excruciating experiences that are outside of a realm children should ever half to endure. And these experiences factor into the anxiety, depression, and suicidal ideations that are presented within the book. One character lives within a physically abusive home. Another character, while not physically abused, is evidently emotionally abused. And a third, sexually assaulted by a person she knows. The trauma each of the characters endures leads to choices that cause greater tribulations.

Throughout the book there are glimmers of hope. Some of the glimmer comes from the adults in the characters' lives who are attempting to reach out. However, the characters are so deep in their pain, fears, and anxieties that they overlook the support that is right in front of them. The fears keep the main character from recognizing that there is a support and not someone ready to shame her for the events in her life.

It's so easy to see all the pain in the world because that is what is presented to us in the news. The thing about life, I am a firm believer, is that there are more people in the world who want to help and be kind than there are people who want to create pain. And those people who want to help come in the forms of parents/guardians, friends, teachers, clergy, neighbors, family doctors, mental health therapists, and in some cases strangers.

There are ways to get help when the pain, fear, and anxieties are unmanaged. You just need to reach out and keep reaching out until you find the person that WILL help. It is a fact that people who reach out for help do get better and in some cases recover. The author of *Heaven's Note* did reach out for help. She did let people in to hear her story, and she continues to work on her fears and anxieties to become the best person she can be.

*- Licensed School Counselor*

## The following are other ways to help yourself or the person who needs the help:

- First and foremost, "Be Kind: Everyone you meet is fighting a hard battle."

- Be aware of Warning Signs for Suicide: ACT on the FACTS.
  - Acknowledge, Care, and Tell an Adult
  - F.A.C.T. Warning Signs: Feelings, Actions, Changes, Threats.

- Talk to your school counselor or teachers about lessons that could be taught about suicide awareness and prevention.

- Access Suicide Prevention Lifeline: The National Suicide Prevention Lifeline is a 24-hour, toll-free suicide prevention service available to anyone in suicidal crisis. If you need help, please dial: 1-800-273-TALK (8255).

- Access HOPELINE: Text "HOPELINE" to 741741 or go to www.CenterForSuicideAwareness.org for 24/7 free trained crisis counselors.

- Access The Trevor Lifeline: 1-866-488-7386 A national organization focused on crisis and suicide prevention efforts among LGBT youth.

- Keep talking with people when those feelings of pervasive sadness and depression set in. Please keep talking and trust that there are kind people who want to help! You're worth it.

*I was at the precipice of death. I leaned over the edge and took in the scent of the river breeze and listened to the excruciating thunder of the waves that were interminable. There were seconds before I would launch myself into those threatening waters far below. I knew that all of the pain and misery would finally be terminated.*

# Chapter 1

Everyone was scrambling to get to their classes. Students were running and tumbling through the thin, crowded halls of Mend Wood Junior High.

"Melody!" I was startled as I heard my best friend, Autumn, call to me from across the hall.

"Hey, Autumn, can't talk right now. I am going to be late for class! Talk to you later!" I shouted as I turned my brisk walk into a full on sprint. I couldn't talk to her, not after what she did. I knew it was to help me and was only to benefit me. But what she doesn't get is that nobody would understand, and my whole family is going to be put at risk because of her actions.

As I walked into my 4th hour U.S. History class, I was welcomed with a ceremonial applaud. The whole class was staring at me and clapping their hands in my honor.

"Um, what is this about?" I asked in a quiet mumble.

"Well, you got the highest score on the exam last Wednesday!" my teacher Ms. Crowell exclaimed. A grin formed on my face, and I noticed everyone else's smile as well. I was completely shocked, as this was an absolute surprise. I have never been applauded before for something academic. My grades were solid C's, and as if being criticized by my parents wasn't enough, my teachers would completely call me out in front of the whole class for the bad grades I had received. They'd call it "demonstrating the result when you don't put full effort into your work". But honestly, how was I supposed to focus on school and all of that stupid stuff when I have my own struggles going on that are causing me turmoil? I just can't keep up with everything! I didn't want to ponder on this for a while, because either way I got the highest score. I am sure that my parents will be very proud. *They might even take me out to a special dinner! Or finally give me an allowance! Or maybe they would allow me to get a phone. Honestly, what 13 year old doesn't have a phone?*

"Melody?" My mind suddenly slipped back into reality. "Oh, yeah. Sorry. Thank you so much. This is a big surprise!"

"For me as well," Ms. Crowell responded.

I accepted my praise and headed to my desk. I took a seat in the red solid chair next to Max, a kid who is always getting on my nerves and making up some kind of random joke to irritate me. I set my huge, cumbersome pile of school work on my desk that was crooked at an angle and began to work on Section 1-3 of *United States History*.

From the back of my mind, I could feel thoughts creeping up to the surface. These thoughts were so dark and reminded me of only my terrors. Once the thoughts were there, they didn't go away for a while. I tried counting to ten. *1... 2... 3... 4... 5... 6... 7... 8... 9... 10...* Nothing, the thoughts were still coming closer. I was desperate to distract myself. My day had been going well, and these memories would cause me pain for the rest of the day.

"Psst, Melody." I lifted my eyes off my book and looked in the direction of Max.

"What is it now Max!?"

"Did you know that..." He paused for a moment. "You look like a swollen grape or something?"

"What? What do you mean by that Max? I am seriously sick of you little immature jokes."

"No, I didn't mean to offend you. I was talking about those bruises."

"Where?" I asked. Then it all hit me. I looked down on my bare legs and right beneath the line where my shorts end, there was a big black and blue bruise about the size of my hand.

My face suddenly went into a blank and dull expression. My eyes were turning dark and I became frozen. Thoughts started rushing through my head like a twister that was interminable. It just kept going and kept hurting.

"So.."

"Yeah, I- I don't know how I got that."

"What about the one on your ankle?"

"Oh, I forgot about that," I said in a dull whisper. I couldn't handle any more of this conversation. It was way too awkward. How am I supposed to tell him the truth? I can't. I can't dare to tell a single soul because if anyone knew I would be absolute toast. Burnt toast and punished to the maximum.

Thankfully the phone interrupted the awkward conversation with Max.

"Yes, Melody is here," Ms. Crowell said softly into the phone. I suddenly became very shaky and felt like a huge gust of wind had blown over me. The feeling was terrifying. Before I could even finish my thought, the kind, red headed, curly haired teacher, Ms. Crowell, tapped me on the shoulder.

"Mrs. Langer wants to speak with you in her office." I nodded in reply and collected my things, then headed out of the classroom, not knowing when I would return.

# Chapter 2

My stomach was turned inside out. I ached as I put my things in my locker and headed to Mrs. Langer's office. Mrs. Langer is the 8th grade school counselor here at Mend Wood. She is a beautiful listener and respects everyone. Her vibes are truly magical. She puts you in this state of mind where you feel you can be honest no matter what. Granted, I have only talked to her once. That was when Autumn and I were in a big conflict. Why did she want to see me? Did I do something wrong?

Then it dawned on me, Autumn. This is because of Autumn. She told me she had said something and this is it. It is happening right here and right now. I could run and hide in the bathroom, or I could ditch school. No, I couldn't do that. That would lead to a worse punishment when I got home. There was nothing I could do to prevent this from happening. I was in a big muddle.

"Melody, come take a seat." Her room smelled strongly of a fresh lavender. The calm music in the background put my mind at ease a little bit. The carpet had a soft bounce to it as I walked to the padded blue chair to take my seat.

"So, your friend Autumn spoke to me."

"Yes, she told me."

"Do you know what she said, Melody?"

"Yeah. But it is not what you think," I responded with a hint of faultiness in my voice.

"It isn't? I usually don't start a conversation telling you right at the beginning, but she said something about bruises." I gulped a painful mouthful of saliva.

"Can you tell me more about these bruises? Is someone hurting you?"

"No," I answered.

"You can be completely honest in here, Melody. You don't have to be afraid. This is a safe place."

I couldn't keep it in. "No one is hurting me!" I snapped back at her. For the first time, she had tried to push me to reveal the truth. She wanted me to say that someone was hurting me. That there was a reason for the scars and bruises all over my body. There was a reason for my endless crying and painful memories; but I couldn't tell her. I couldn't be honest. It would completely wreck my already imperfect, screwed up family.

"There is no need to have this poor attitude and no need to snap at me."

"Well, you are pushing me to say something that is not true!"

"I have a little secret power Melody. I can tell when someone might be lying."

"Well, I am not! So stop accusing me of lying." I'd had enough of this crap. I just wanted to run out of this room and cry.

"Okay then, there is nothing else for us to talk about. If you talk back to a teacher like that again, then we will give you a slip and a call home. But I am going to let this one slide as it may have been an uncomfortable position for you to be in." I snatched the pink pass out of her hand and ran out of the office, slamming the door behind me.

I was shocked at myself. I cannot believe that I let my

behavior go too far. I do feel bad. Very bad, I feel so guilty. I shouldn't have snapped at her. It's just the position she put me in. I know she doesn't believe what I had told her. I know my problem. I am too analytical. I overthink *everything and this is just another example of that. I am over thinking things right now. This very moment.* I rushed out of the Student Services area where Mrs. Langer's office was and dashed all the way to the hallway where I was greeted by a herd of students anxious to get to their next class. I clipped the corner and went sprinting into the girl's bathroom. After what felt like an eternity running, I had finally gotten there. I locked myself into the second bathroom stall.

I curled up into a little ball on top of the toilet seat so that if anyone came in they couldn't see me. This stall is like my happy place, but not so happy. There is graffiti all over the stall. When I retreat here, I like reading the often funny puns, jokes, or drawings written on the walls. There is always something new every day. It helps me to calm down a little, though recently it stopped working. It only made my problems worse.

I had this obsessive need to scream, which I wanted to compulse on, but I didn't. It would draw way too much attention to the tiny blue stall in the girl's bathroom. Tears started forming in my eyes as I stared down at those swollen bruises noticeable to everyone. Mrs. Langer knew I was lying. *What if she contacts social services? My parents would never forgive me. I can't believe that my best friend would go and report that I have an "unusual" amount of bruises without asking me! Like she was assuming the very worst.* My whole body was trembling, my breathing was heavy, my vision had become blurry and I could feel fatigue washing over me like a whole swarm of bees attacking and making me faint.

My breathing continued to get heavier and it felt like my heart was going to burst out of my bruised chest, which was the only place there were bruises people couldn't see. Tears were now down my cheeks and trickling down my jaw. My nose was all stuffed up. I jumped when I heard the bell for the next class. I wanted to leave the little stall and act like everything was alright. Like I wasn't crying, like I wasn't so scared of my own home, like I wasn't that one girl with bruises all over her body.

I know people wonder. I have been approached several times. The same exact questions every time. *"What happened?" "Are you okay?"* On the rare occasion, even asking me if I was being abused. I just wish Autumn had asked me instead of reporting it. I could have made an excuse like I fell off my bike, or I tripped down the stairs. *Not like that doesn't happen to me like all the time already.*

I knew I had to get my courage ignited and head to class. I slowly took some of the insanely rough and thin toilet paper and dried my eyes. The tears had soaked through and my fingers were wet. The minute I unlocked the blue stall door, my nose cleared up. I could smell the nasty odor coming from the stall next to me. I went up to the twin sinks and looked in the very dirty mirror. My eyes were swollen and puffy. They had red shadowing them and you could still tell where tears were trailing down my cheeks. I washed the glossy and radiant tear marks off of my cheeks and tried to make my eyes look "normal". That didn't work out too well. Regardless of how bad my puffy face and swollen bruises looked, I decided to head to my next class.

Before I walked into my 5th hour, I grabbed a pencil and erased the time on my late pass and changed it to 11:33 a.m., the present time.

"Melody Potter, you are late again," my English teacher scowled in an abrupt manner.

"I have a pass, Mrs. Welsh."

"That's a first. Very well then, have a seat. We are silently reading. Quickly set down your stuff and join the rest of the class. I hope you brought a book Ms. Potter."

I dug through the clutter in my bag and found my book, *The Last Time We Say Goodbye*. The book was about a young teenager whose brother committed suicide. It gives me nostalgia from the "suicide talk" Mrs. Langer gave a couple months ago.

*"Good afternoon class, I am Mrs. Langer, your lovely guidance counselor, just in case you forgot who I was. Today, we are going to be talking about a very serious matter, suicide. Believe it or not, suicide is a very real thing happening in our community. We've had several attempts by students from this school as a matter of fact. But I shall not say any names. Bringing awareness to this, I will inform you on the clear and sometimes not lucid warning signs that someone might be considering suicide or going through some hard times."*

Anyway, you get the point. I am truly enjoying this book because it shows a different perspective on suicide and how it can affect others emotionally, and academically.

# Chapter 3

I stared down at my blue wrist watch and looked at the time, 12:29. One more minute until lunch. As the bell rang once the clock hit 12:30, I rushed to pack up my things and pushed in my chair. I rushed out of the room as fast as possible. I had to make sure that I caught up to Autumn before she went to that old, and way too over crowded lunch room, which I cannot stand because it triggers my social anxiety majorly.

"Autumn!" I screamed out to her as I saw her locking her tall, tan locker shut. She turned her head and started walking in my direction at a brisk pace.

"What's up Melody? Why were you in such a race to get to class this morning?"

"You have caused me a lot of stress Autumn. Just know that."

"What do you mean? About the bruises? Are you angry with me?"

"Yes Autumn! You should have asked me when you saw them instead of reporting them and telling me last minute!" I shouted directly into her face.

Her expression immediately drew into a relished face. The kind she gets when she is extremely angry.

"I was trying to help you!" she snarled in a defensive way. "Sorry, I wanted to help my friend. You shouldn't be angry! If someone is hurting you," her voice became more solemn and emotional, "then you need to talk to someone. I know how this can affect someone, you know, my own cousin, Brandon."

"You didn't need to report it though Autumn." I didn't want to go through another fight with her. I know we both are to blame in this conflict, but all I want is an apology.

If she only knew how much turmoil her words and actions had caused, about the anxiety I suffered from, and the breakdown I'd had today in the girls bathroom.

"You're right, Melody. I am not going to say that I'm at fault completely in this, but I am sorry. I never meant to hurt you."

"Me too, Autumn," I apologized, still a little bit infuriated by the conflict. But I didn't want this to get worse. Autumn is my only friend.

"Can we please head to lunch now, Melody?" Autumn asked, interrupting my thoughts.

"Sure," I responded.

As we made our way slowly through the halls, I could tell Autumn didn't completely mean her apology. I know she would never deliberately hurt my feelings or try to go against my wishes. But she did this because she was really worried about me and probably still is.

My social anxiety was immediately triggered once we walked into the cafeteria. I could smell the horrid scent of the school's hot dogs and I heard the clatter of silverware. Everyone was talking in such a weird manner. It felt as if they were all talking about me. Like they were noticing my bruises, like they heard about my breakdown, or worse, they somehow knew the truth. I could feel their eyes watching me like hawks. Looking me up and down, judging every single detail about me. From my ugly peach colored shoes to the fly-aways in my brown curly hair.

"Hey, are you okay?" Autumn must have noticed I was getting anxious about this whole social situation.

"Yeah, I'm fine. I'm going to go find a seat."

"Okay, I'll be there in a little bit," Autumn responded.

I trailed over to the empty seats right next to the window, and as far away from everyone else as possible. As I waited for Autumn to return with her lunch, I stared at a giant weeping willow tree swaying in the graceful wind of this cool fall day. It was mesmerizing. If only I could look at this every single time I start to get nervous or depressed. It really calms my nerves.

"You need to start talking about those bruises though." I was startled to hear Autumn's voice. I hadn't realized that she had sat down right next to me at the gray speckled lunch table.

"Why do I need to talk about it?"

"Because you got them somehow, now spill." I didn't know what to say. "I- I, um, got them by falling. I fell down the stairs," I stuttered.

"That doesn't seem believable Melody." Care had immediately ignited in her voice, and her eyes were violently bare, staring at my bruises. I could tell. She could see right through me. She must know the horrid truth.

# Chapter 4

My day was so chaotic, awful really. It was filled with anxiety, tears and yelling. I got off the bus and started walking towards my tiny blue house in the neighborhood of way too small townhouses. My mom and dad were home. It was obvious by their only vehicle, a rusty blue sedan, being parked in the driveway. Blue probably isn't the best word to describe it. It was brown due to the immense amount of dirt and mud on it. I noticed how the driveway had some tar damage because of the many severe thunderstorms. I walked up my steps, fearing what was to happen next. I opened up the front door and was greeted by a holler.

"Melody! What have you done?!?"

"Excuse me, ma?"

"Uh, we got a phone call from your school counselor today! What is this about us abusing you?!?!" my father exclaimed. He was starting to get mad, no infuriated.

"I swear, I never said anything about you abusing me!" I answered in a more civil tone.

"Well, she thinks you are lying! You are worthless Melody!" my mother hollered.

My dad had disappeared into the hallway. My mother was staring at me violently. My dad peeked back in through the hallway with a brown leather belt in his hand and his expression said that I needed to be ready for yet another beating. Tears made a stream down my face as I got whipped with the belt on my chest. The belt slapped and dragged across my chest quick drawing blood, leaving a thick line where the belt had hit. Excruciating pain had swelled over me almost immediately.

I fell to the floor, gasping for air. You could taste the deep smoke in the air, and it hurt to inhale it in. My lungs choked on the secondhand smoke that had filled them. It felt like a whole minute even though it was a matter of seconds. And the pain would last forever. It was only one whip, and that was it. *Thank God.*

My dad threw the belt across the room.

"Now you are going to assure Mrs. Langer tomorrow that we do not abuse you!" he screamed, lowering his tone a small, teeny bit. "If you don't, you know what is coming for you," he threatened.

*Yeah, I'll tell Mrs. Langer that you TOTALLY don't abuse me. 110 percent!*

I briskly walked down the hall to my room. I shut the door behind me and jumped on my poorly made bed. I was lucky to even have a home, food, clothes, and a bed. But that doesn't make up for the horrors that lie behind the dark blue walls of the house behind the white picket fence surrounding our yard. Behind the old damp wooden door. I clenched my jaw in pain; tears made a river down my face. No, a lake would be more accurate. What did I do to deserve this? I was bleeding through my white tank top and I could already see the purple splotches forming a bruise as I lifted my shirt to check the damage. Yet another bruise. I sunk deep into my mattress and buried my head into my pillow to muffle out my crying. I could feel the pain inside of me boiling up to a temperature so hot, I could feel my heart racing, the thoughts contemplating inside my head. I felt like there was absolutely no escape. I was stuck in an endless hole of darkness and despair. And it seemed like it would never end. It lasts all the time, everyday, and nobody knows. I am trapped in my own mind.

***

I must have fallen asleep while crying because I woke up to a glimpse of sun peeking through my curtains in my dark and lonely room. I stared at my watch. My alarm was about to go off in a couple of minutes. I turned off my alarm and arose from my bed to get dressed. It would be no surprise that my parents wouldn't be awake. They always like to sleep in, and I depend on myself. All they ever do is make sure I have shelter, yell and scream at me, beat me, and make sure there are necessities in the house. I have to make my own food, wake up on my own, do a lot of the housework, and fend for myself basically.

They haven't always been like this, however. My parents used to be kind and loving. They would make me dinner every single night, read me bedtime stories, and hug and kiss me good night. It all changed a couple of years ago. It was a tragic event that shaped the rest of my future.

*"Mrs. and Mr. Potter, we are sorry to call you at such a late time of day, but we have some rather tragic news. There was an accident and Mrs. Potter's parents were involved. We are sorry to say that the outcome of the collision on Highway 96 had no survivors. Do you want to plan a funeral?"*

It happened just like that. They got a phone call, and that was it. Their whole world had come crumbling down, and all that was left was a closed casket and a burial ground surrounded with tulips, my grandparents' favorite flower. They didn't even have a funeral. My parents decided it was too expensive. I loved and cherished my grandparents. They were my only grandparents. My other set had died before

I was born. They were amazing to me. I can't help but think to myself that if they had not died, I wouldn't be in this state I am right now. My parents wouldn't have so much anger they feel the need to take it out on me, and they wouldn't be so depressed. Our life has changed drastically from this. I just don't quite understand why suddenly I have become the victim in their turmoil.

I finished getting dressed. I decided to wear jeans that cover up my bruises and tennis shoes to cover up the bruise on my ankle. I quietly crept out of my room and to the bathroom, being extra circumspect to not disturb my parents and wake them. As I flashed on the bathroom lights, I was shocked by what had been left for me. There was a note written to me by my mother.

*My dearest Melody, you must not show this to your father. This must be kept a secret. Do not tell anyone and do not show anyone. This is an apology from the bottom of my heart. I have caused you tremendous and indescribable pain. You have suffered because of your father and I. I am so sorry that I haven't done anything to intercept the abuse. I am sorry. It is getting harder each day. My bruises keep adding up as yours do. He does not like me. He hates me. He despises me. He doesn't love you either. I do! I love you more than the world and nothing can change that. I should have risked my own life to interfere with the abuse. I should have ignored his threats to help you, my loving daughter. The death of your grandparents shocked both of us. Your father was very angry because of this death. The resentment he has toward us isn't because of us specifically. It is from the many reasons why the death of your grandparents was a life changer. You are too young to understand why your father is so angry*

*because of the death. It is not because a cherished*
*family member died, and it's not for financial reasons.*
*In time, you will know the truth. Keep searching.*
*I can't tell you because I won't be around much longer.*
*This is my goodbye honey. My sweet and loving Melody,*
*I wish I could kiss you goodbye.*

Before I even finished reading this letter I was in tears. My mother actually loved me. She actually cared about me. She had empathy for me. I was so confused though. And what did she mean by this is goodbye?

I sprinted out of the lit up bedroom and rushed at full speed into my parents' bedroom.

I knocked first, no answer. I solemnly turned the round and rusted door handle and what I saw was truly terrifying. My mother's limp body lay on the ground in a puddle of blood, as my father lay passed out on the bed with a gun in the palm of his hands, and shattered beer bottles all around him.

I heard a sudden but quiet beep. It continued to ring softly in my ear before I awoke to a gentle tap.

***

"Miss Potter?"

I softly fluttered my eyes. The scent of cleanliness was strong and vivid. The dull pale room reminded me of a scene from a horror movie.

"Hello. Where am I?" I whispered in a frightened, yet calm manner.

"Melody Potter, you are in Mend Wood Hospital."

I looked around the dull hospital room. I stared at the heart monitor. That must have been the solid beeping noise I had heard.

"What- where am I-"

"It's okay Melody. You are safe here. An officer will be in with you soon to speak to you."

"Oka-a-ay," I muttered in response, hints of confusion in my voice.

I saw the nurse quietly walk out of the room. The whole place was terrifying to me. I had never been in a hospital room before. Thoughts were taking over my mind and swirling like a twister. I felt completely hopeless, and utterly confused. What had happened? How did I end up in this big muddle and old hospital room?

My mind exited out my thoughts once I heard a loud and startling knock on the door to my room. I dried my tears that were forming a river down my face as I watched the middle aged police officer carry his cumbersome bags to a taller chair next to my bed.

"This must have been a tiring day for you Melody."

"Ye-s," I stammered.

"I am Mike O'Neil. I am on the Mend Wood Police force. Do you know why I am here?"

I shook my head. I envied the strength in his voice. Maybe if I knew why I was here in this solitary hospital room I would be able to have a bit of strength in my voice too. Instead, I sat there like a clueless bird.

"Do you remember your mother?"

"My mother?" I responded. My mind had a sudden switch. I blinked my eyes a couple of times and I remembered…

*I could feel my toes curling into the carpeted floor. I could feel the streaks of tears on my face of disappointment and sorrows. I lifted my head up from being tucked in beneath my bruised legs and stared at my mother's bare and limp body on the floor in the pool of blood. It was a hideous sight to see. My mind was trying to comprehend why my mother was lying dead on the floor. Was it suicide? Murder? I arose from the ground and started to walk around toward the front of her. I stared down at her closed eyelids, waiting for her to flutter them and show a sign of life. But I knew she was nonviable. I moved my gaze over to her neck, and other limbs. They were completely covered in bruises. I didn't want to come to the conclusion, but I know it was true, my father had killed my mother. That is what she meant in the letter. All of the emotions of anger, despair, frustration, and disappointment were rushing through my whole being. I rushed to the phone and simply dialed 9-1-1.*

*"9-1-1, what is your emergency?"*

*"My mother she- she- she is dead," I stammered.*

*"Address?"*

*"137 Mount Ridge Circle"*

*"Can you tell us what happened sweetie?"*

*"My, um, my da- dad beat her to death."*

*By now, tears were forming puddles beneath my eyes once again.*

*"We are sending services right now. They will be there in a few minutes. Where is your father right now?"*

*"He is, pass- passed out," I said in a whimper.*

*"Stay calm sweetie. Do not wake up your father. Lock yourself in another room and do not let anyone in until you hear our first responders. Do you understand?"*

*"Yes."*

*"Stay on the line with me. Tell me if you hear your father wake up."*

*The lady's voice soothed my emotions a little bit. I quickly locked myself in the bathroom, still holding on the house phone. I leaned one ear against the door to make sure that I could hear when the first responders got here and if my dad was to wake up.*

"Melody? Do you remember what happened to your mother, Elizabeth Potter?" I snapped back to reality in a flash. "Yes, my father beat her to death."

"Do you remember what happened after that?"

"I, um, called 9-1-1 and followed the directions of the operator," I responded.

"Anything after that? Do you remember the first responders arriving at your house?"

### The Rest of It

Melody heard the knock of what she thought was the first responders. To her surprise, it was her arrogant father. Melody opened the wooden bathroom door and was immediately slammed to the floor. Her father hit her in the head with a metal baseball bat. The crashing sound was horrific. The anger that rushed through him encouraged him to swing more at his daughter's limp arms and legs.

"Stop right there! Police! Drop the weapon!"

Mr. Potter took one more swing until he followed the order of the officer and dropped the bat. The officers sprinted toward him and cuffed him. Melody was put onto a stretcher and immediate care was done on her while they drove away in the fleet of police cars with her father in the barred back seat. Her mother, meanwhile, was being taken away to the morgue.

# Chapter 5

"**M**elody, do you remember your father beating you up?"

"What time?" I asked hesitantly. Part of my clueless brain thought that they knew about the abuse.

"How many times has he abused you sweetie?"

"Why?'

"I know you have a history of being deceitful when it comes to your father. You don't have to be afraid. He cannot hurt you now. He is incarcerated. Can you come to tell me the truth even in this dismal room?"

"Three times a week," I said.

" Could you elaborate?"

"He, my father, would abuse me at least three times a week. Whenever I disobeyed him or did something against his morals, he would abuse me."

"How so?"

"You know, punch me, hit me, kick me. He mostly whipped me though with his belt."

"Okay. Do you know what he did to you today?"

"I, I, didn't think he did anything," I responded.

"He beat you up. You were unconscious. That is why you are here right now."

It all started to make sense. I still couldn't exactly remember when and how he beat me up, but it suddenly explained the fresh and forming bruises and the aches and swelling

I was experiencing. My voice to the officer sounded strong and well. I seemed fine, but inside, I was dying. I could never have guessed that my own father would kill my mother. I have had the thoughts, but never believed he would actually do it.

After the officer left with my statement the nurse strolled in to give me an update. She said that I would be out by tomorrow and then I would go into a group home for girls. With no known living relatives, it is impossible to stay at my house. Apparently, the group home I will be moving to is only a before and after school program. I will go to school like usual, yippie, and then go back to the group home.

A few hours later, I had met with this very kind social worker named Mary. She assured me that I would find a loving and kind foster family in the neighborhood, but until then I will be in this group home for other kids like me. I will be in group therapy sessions with other kids who have experienced "trauma" as well there. She never explained in detail what will happen to my father. Most likely prison, for life. He was being charged with 2nd degree murder.

I used to wonder how it was possible for someone's whole life to change in a matter of one day or minutes. Now I understand. In one night, my mother was beaten all the way down to the hardwood and bare floor where she took her last breath. In a morning, my father beat me up to unconsciousness and was arrested. And in a whole day, I end up in the hospital getting ready to move to a group home. My life has forever turned upside down, and I don't know how I will ever escape the misery this life is piling on me.

# Chapter 6

I awoke to the sound of a peaceful bird humming outside the window. The room was beautifully lit up with sunshine and was glistening, radiant and true. I stretched my arms and pulled off my blanket. I looked over across the room and saw Caitlyn. The beautiful humming was actually coming from my roommate here at Woods Group Home for Girls. Caitlyn had the most beautiful auburn hair and vibrant green eyes. Her voice sounded like an angel.

"Good morning Caitlyn."

"Good morning Melody. How did you sleep last night?"

"I slept actually pretty well," I responded with a smile.

"I sure hope your first day wasn't too bad here!"

"It wasn't at all. I am glad to be here. I don't have to be scared all of the time," I responded. It was true, I didn't have to be frightened that something awful would happen, that my life would spiral down past rock bottom, if that was even possible.

"I totally get that. I was completely scared of being at my old house because of all of the males. They make me nervous. Because, well, you know."

"Yeah. You don't need to talk about it," I responded with a gentle and genuine tone in my voice.

Caitlyn was the absolute kindest and most appreciative girl here at Woods. She has the soft kind of voice that soothes you and her story touches the hearts of everyone who hears it.

It all started when Caitlyn was 10. Her uncle had raped her. Since then, she developed social anxiety around all men. You know, thinking they were having fantasies about her or staring at her excessively, dreaming and plotting for a way to enter Caitlyn's "personal" being. Caitlyn then developed PTSD and severe depression. She didn't want anyone else to go through what she was going through, so she started a campaign, #StopSexualAbuse. She ended up hosting fundraisers and earned thousands of dollars to help support kids in foster care, or in treatment because of sexual abuse issues. She is truly amazing and inspirational. I just wish that I could do something that spectacular to make a difference in this world. But instead I am just the kid in foster care because her father is a child abuser and a murderer, and her own mother is lying in a grave. I will never be worthy enough or have the potential to really make a positive difference in this world. Or at least it feels like that.

Amber Lee Grayson is the head of Woods. She is sophisticated and strict. She doesn't let anything be condoned. From what I heard from the other girls, she can be visciously rude and mean. She likes to ridicule her least favorites and praise whom she admires most, which you can guess was Caitlyn. As for me, she didn't seem to mind my insecure and depressed personality. She was kind to me, but wasn't the most happy that I was there. Rachel is another girl here. She is super kind to everyone. Her story is less dramatic and exciting, but Amber Lee absolutely despises Rachel, for no apparent reason.

"Girls! Come downstairs for breakfast and then off to school!" I could hear Amber Lee's holler from all the way upstairs through the shut door. I didn't know how she would react if I came down late, so Caitlyn and I headed straight downstairs. I could smell the melted butter on the golden and fluffy pancakes that were stacked in a neat and orderly row as I stumbled my way down the wooden stairs. The maple syrup was in a fancy pitcher and seven plates were elegantly placed in a circle around the pitcher. Pitchers of milk, apple juice, and orange juice lined the sides of the grand, furnished table.

"Good morning Amber Lee. This all looks so delicious!" I exclaimed.

"Thank you, Melody. I hope you enjoy this fine meal."

"I am sure I will. I haven't eaten like this in years!" And that was true. I always stuck to eating an apple or a granola bar for breakfast. My parents would never make me something as elegant as this, or anything at all to be truthful. This is why this is such a momentous occasion for me and I want to append a good and positive attitude onto it!

"Melody, want to sit by me?" Caitlyn asked in her soft murmur.

"Absolutely!" I responded.

Once all of the girls arrived, we started to mow down all of the scrumptious food until our plates were shiny and clean.

"Now girls, today is Melody's first day back at Mend Wood Middle School, so let's remember confidentiality to support and have manners with Melody. If anyone asks anything personal to any of you about Melody or yourselves, simply tell them it is none of their business and walk away. Remember to look out for each other whenever possible," Amber Lee proclaimed.

We put all of our dirty dishes in the sink and cleaned the table. Once that was all done we packed our bags for school and we were out the door in a flash.

The "special" bus arrived to pick us up at the end of the driveway of what seemed like a group home mansion. It was a smaller bus, one for only students in group homes, hospitals, or the disabled. I felt so embarrassed to be brought to school in this bus. Everybody would know I was some kind of messed up kid.

We arrived at the school within minutes. I walked into the building and headed for my locker. I put the combo into my dull and rusted locker, and grabbed all of my materials for my first hour class with Mrs. Johnson. When I got there, I left my belongings in the classroom and headed out looking for Autumn. It wasn't long until I found her, lingering at her locker, rummaging through her cumbersome pile of things.

"Hey, Autumn," I said to her with a slight grin on my face.

"Hey Melody! Oh my gosh I missed you soo much!"

"I missed you too. Let me explain-"

"No need to explain. It is all over the news. It is okay. I am here for you now," Autumn interrupted.

Autumn's words seemed inspirational to me. She actually cared, but part of me felt entirely exposed and vulnerable. The whole school knows what had happened, not all the bits of detail, but they know and it scares me half to death.

I could just imagine them talking behind my back, gossiping. *Can you believe her own father murdered her mother? What a loser of a family!"* I tried to hold my breath and ignore the thoughts going through my head. The bell was about to ring in less than a minute, so I decided to say my goodbyes to Autumn and head to my first hour.

Before I even made it to Mrs. Johnson's 1st hour class Mrs. Langer stopped me in my tracks. "Good morning Melody," she said.

"Good morning Mrs. Langer," I stammered.

"Will you come into my office?"

"Sure," I responded. A whole wave of anxiety suddenly washed over me. She knew I lied to her. She knows what happened. What was she going to say to me? I softly wandered into the dark yet pleasing office and breathed in the fresh lavender smell. I gently took a seat on a blue chair and listened to Mrs. Langer speak.

"I am so sorry for all the turmoil you have been experiencing Melody."

"Thanks," I mumbled.

"I know this must be incredibly hard for you. You have suffered a great loss. You were ripped away from your family."

"Yeah," I could feel tears forming in my eyes. "I never thought that everything could change so much in just one night. My whole life has shifted." My voice was quiet and sort of high pitched.

Mrs. Langer could tell that I was extremely emotional. It was all true. My whole life had shifted within one night. I feel empty inside. I have lost everything and everyone I called family. I am alone.

"Before we talk a little more, I would like to inform you of a few support groups I think you would be interested in here at the school. First, is a loss and grief support group that I run. I also run a support group for kids like you who have been abused. You don't have to make up your mind now, but if you are interested they will be starting in October."

That was just a short month away. I think part of me was interested. I don't want to feel alone like this anymore. "I am interested."

"Great. I will give you more information in a few weeks. So… tell me… anything you think I should know?"

"Well," I started, "I just want to say I am incredibly sorry for lying to you. My dad has abused me several times, all the time, and I didn't want to tell anyone because I wouldn't be safe." I just had to tell her the truth. Guilt had been whirling over me and weighing me down ever since I lied to her. Lying isn't in my nature.

"Understandable Melody. I am glad you finally came out and told the truth."

"Well, I kind of had to, you know, after I found my mother… dead." By this point tears were completely making a stream down my face. My whole body felt limp and bare. I felt so exposed. This is the first time I have been able to truly say what I am feeling to someone who actually cares, like Mrs. Langer. I don't think the social workers or medical workers cared at all. They were all helping me for the money, that was all. Mrs. Langer can almost see into my soul. She could tell when I was lying, and she wants to be aware of what had happened. I appreciate it.

"Melody, it's okay. Your dad can't hurt anyone now. You are safe. There is hope. You are worthy and you can be brave. You will fight through this," Mrs. Langer said in a whisper, gently placing her hand on my shoulder.

"Thank you," I said.

I took a few deep breaths and Mrs. Langer decided to speak again. "In a way, are you a little bit glad that this all happened? If it hadn't of happened, you would still be in danger."

I hesitated. "Yes, kind of, sort of, only a little bit."

"Well, it is okay Melody. I will be working with your group home and will help you through this hard time. If there is anything you ever need, do not hesitate to make an appointment with me. Also, this space is open for you to take breaks if and when you need to, for whenever things get to be too much."

"Thank you Mrs. Langer," I responded as I headed out of the room.

The halls were empty, and the silence struck my mind. It was a sudden feeling of loneliness. I was that strange girl, probably the only person whose father killed her own mother. No one will want to be my friend. I am just that messed up girl. I stared at the tan lockers as I walked and made my way to my 1st hour class. There was absolute dead silence as I entered the room.

"Good morning Melody," Mrs. Johnson exclaimed. "Please have a seat." I trotted to the little red desk in the very far back of the classroom and plopped my things down and put my attention on Mrs. Johnson. Everybody was staring at me with curious and dull eyes. I knew they wanted to ask me about what had happened. I could imagine all of the questions they would ask flying around in my mind. I wouldn't be able to answer them all. I wouldn't want to. Instead of listening to Mrs. Johnson's lecture on exponents, and why math is so important, I brought my attention to doodling in my notebook. I started simply drawing a head curled up in a pair of legs, then I added the hair, clothing, and the shading, making a masterpiece.

# Chapter 7

*She was holding her knees tightly and crying, waiting for the event to begin. Her long black dress had a simple buckled belt, and even though the dress was a piece of absolute lace and beauty, she was very unhappy. Her curled luscious brown hair with streaks of dirty blond were gorgeous, but her beauty couldn't hide the internal pain she was feeling. She lifted her head, eyes all red and swollen, and looked at the wet splotch on her dress stained by tears. It was about to start. She finger combed her hair and tried to put on a brave face as she walked into the room that was filled with friends. She took her seat and stared at the closed wooden casket decorated nicely, and surrounded by roses and tulips. The music was peaceful to her ears, but reminded her deeply of what had been lost, what had been ripped away from her, what she had regretted in her life. She regretted not saying goodbye, not saying, "I love you Mama."*

I couldn't stop the overwhelming feeling of hopelessness, loss, regret. It swarmed around me every day like a tornado that just wouldn't terminate. My mind was full of memories and scars that would never heal, never fade away, and never get a happy ending. It is all over. She is gone. He is gone. I didn't get to say goodbye. Regardless of the abuse, she was still my mother, and she apologized. But I never got the chance to say, "I forgive you Mama," because I do forgive her. I forgive her for the sins. I wish things had turned out differently because now I am without a real family and my mind is a home I am trapped in, and it is lonely inside this mansion.

The funeral was over, the casket was gone, and she was off to get cremated. It was all over, and that was my last chance to say goodbye, but I couldn't. I couldn't have made the tears stop in their tracks down my rosy cheeks and I couldn't have gotten the courage to go up to the casket itself and come to reality that it was over. I walked out of the old and rundown church. I sat on the beautiful benches staring at the florescent glass windows as I waited for Liberty, the new co-leader for Woods, and Amber Lee Grayson to pick me up. The gray sedan pulled up next to the church and Liberty and Amber Lee welcomed me into the little car.

"How was the funeral Melody?" Liberty asked.

"It was... um... I would rather not talk about it," I said as I could feel the tears forming in my eyes once again.

"Melody, you are going to have to talk about it eventually in group therapy today. So think about your feelings and what you would like to share," Amber Lee suggested. I sighed and nodded my head in agreement. I didn't want to do group therapy. It is too uncomfortable. It is hard enough that everyone knows what happened on a broader scale. I just cannot handle them knowing all the details. Knowing that the person who should have loved me and my mother the most abused me and murdered her.

Every single day here they force you to share with everyone. They have forced me to share almost every dreaded detail about my dismal life. And now they want me to share yet again, right after my mom's funeral, the worst time.

As soon as the car pulled up the long and steep driveway I hopped out and quickly trailed up the brick steps to the red cedar building and waited for Amber Lee and Liberty to unlock the door. As soon as I heard the click from the

key, I rushed in and went straight up to my room. Caitlyn
was already there, but it wasn't at all as I expected to see her.

*I was just a baby, a toddler perhaps. Lonely and lost
in the big world people called Earth. My mommy and
daddy were always fighting. I would run up the stairs
and run right back down as soon as I saw the broken
glass, or fresh bruises on my mother's bare body. The soft,
freshly cleaned carpet along the steps of the stairs never
soothed my crying, but did give me a sense of escape. If
I needed to run right back down that staircase, I could,
freely. As I grew up, my brown hair became more
auburn, my eyes became more vibrant and green, and
my mother's hair was growing gray, her whole body
became sore. She died in the next week. Her breast
cancer had made an epidemic throughout her whole
body, and she was gone. I said my goodbyes as I stood
over her crying at the hospice, where she died in my
very arms. As I was hugging her, she was greeting death.
The next weeks and months were dreadful. I was only
an 8 year old, and my mama had passed away. The
great sadness struck me and I hid, I stayed in seclusion.
Locking myself away from all reality and all living life.
I spent days and months sleeping and crying into my
memory foam pillow. Until one day, I heard a thump
at my door. I opened it with caution and two deputies
stood there looking at me with dull expressions and sad
eyes. "Caitlyn Greene, we are sorry to inform you, but
your father has committed suicide this evening. He ran
into ongoing traffic, willingly. Pack up your stuff, we
are here to take you to your uncle's." I was only 8 when
my mother had died from cancer, and 10 when my
dad had ran into ongoing traffic, ending his life, and
abandoning mine. That very day, I rode in the small,*

*crowded and barred down police car to the Oak Wood house where my uncle lived. I wasn't even there a week when he snuck into my room, told me to get undressed and ready for bed, and it happened. He forced me to the bed, unbuckled his jeans, and did it. He raped me. I reported it to my school the next day. He was arrested, and I was put into foster care. And that is my story, and this is why I am writing this note. I cannot keep pretending to be positive and happy, and I can't keep pretending that I didn't get raped, that I didn't get abused, that I don't have PTSD, depression, anxiety. I can't live everyday listening to the echoing sirens of when the officers pulled up and arrested him, I can't keep remembering and repeating the same amount of tears I shed once my mother had passed away. So, this is the end. Thank you Amber Lee, Liberty, and my new friend, Melody. I will always have you guys in my heart. Now that I am gone, I hope I will be in your hearts as well.*

*Goodbye, Caitlyn Greene.*

Blood was spattered all over the floor. The gun lay fallen beside her head and blood kept gushing from the open wound. The note was placed on the desk, and it was too late. While we were all gone at the funeral or school, Caitlyn had committed suicide. I sprawled onto the ground. I lay beside Caitlyn and just screamed. I screamed and cried and moped. Amber Lee came rushing up the stairs, and Liberty wasn't far behind her. They sprinted into the room and saw exactly what I had seen, the bloody mess and unspeakable terror of Caitlyn's dead and limp body. They then unfolded the note with care, and their faces and mine became violently bare.

# Chapter 8

I woke up and listened to the thunder banging against my little glass window. The lightning radiantly shined through the unscathed glass barrier that separated the outside world and me.

My room reeked of death even after the solemn night had passed. The rain dripped from my window and I rested my eyes. I stared over at my backpack, and knew I had to awake to get ready for school. Another dreadful day of school where I would have to face my fears once again, but once and for all.

The bus had been late and left me soaking wet and shivering. The other girls seemed fine with Caitlyn being gone, but it was just another loss for me, and I couldn't bear the pain of it. I sat down upon my white knit sweater to avoid getting the bus seats wet, and listened calmly to the rain tapping against the window. The blue droplets that trickled down the window reminded me solemnly of my own self. My blue and drilled up spirit, and my loss of energy and excitement.

The school had seemed normal, regular. No one seemed to notice the loss of a valued community member, probably because she didn't go to our school, but they must have heard the news. And Caitlyn was so well known. She was so kind, and beautiful.

I didn't feel like finding Autumn. I didn't feel like talking to Mrs. Langer. I just felt like curling up in a blanket and escaping into my own terrifying thoughts.

Caitlyn seemed so brave. She seemed together, positive, happy. It never occurred to us that she might be still feeling depressed, anxious, or even suicidal. We were dumb to not have thought that her trauma still affects her day to day, and haunts her thoughts. We should have looked for the warning signs, should have spotted them before she got driven too far, and now she is gone. She can never be returned, and it is sickening.

The day felt like it was just beginning, like it was just starting, like a whole new world was being created. I went from class to class, held my head down low, and thought about what was to come in the next hours. My backpack was ready. I had a flashlight, granola bars, spare clothing, a small blanket, a few water bottles, a pocket knife, and my life's savings, $35. I was prepared to head out, head out of this town, of this city, the little and frightening town of Mend Wood. I was ready to go on an adventure and leave this town forever. And all I had to do was get Autumn on board.

It was 9th period, the very last period of the day, and my very last period at Mend Wood, I was sure of it. Before class started, I headed down to Mrs. Langer's office. She was peacefully sitting down at her desk, and the smell of lavender brought back nostalgia.

"Mrs. Langer?" I whispered, peeking into her office.

"Yes, Melody, how are you?"

"Holding together, I guess. I just wanted to say thank you for everything. Thank you for your kind words, helpful advice, and this space. I have to go. Goodbye. Goodbye for a long time Mrs. Langer." I quickly trailed out of the room and headed back to my locker. I knew she would call me back down to her office after that, so I immediately grabbed my backpack and headed for Autumn's 9th period class.

I creaked open the door, brutally interrupting a conversation on Shakespeare. "Can I speak to Autumn quickly?" I asked.

Her teacher, Mr. Richards, responded with, "What is this for?"

"Another class," I quickly stuttered.

"Alright then, Autumn, be back soon," he responded. I could tell that Autumn was extremely worried and confused. The expression on her face told a whole story of anxiety on its own. I hadn't showed up to lunch today, so as far as Autumn knew I wasn't here at all today. But I needed lunch time to write out my plan of action.

Autumn closed the door behind her and we walked out into the area of the school that was filled with brand new blue lockers and white and bright green futons.

"What is this about Melody?" Autumn said with concern and empathy in her voice.

"Listen to me, we are leaving. Don't speak until I am done talking. We are running away. We need to do this. We can't live here anymore, well at least I can't. But I cannot live without my best friend. You need to come with me. We are just going to leave and not tell anyone. It will be a secret. But we have to leave now-"

"Woah! Melody, stop! I cannot just leave my parents!"

"Yes you can," I suggested. "You just need to leave, it will be okay. You said you didn't like your parents that much anyway. All they ever do is emotionally abuse you, so what's holding you back from this adventure?"

"Umm, you are right, kind of, there isn't anything holding me back, but this is my home Melody, my parents, my life." Autumn seemed reluctant, but I could tell she was gaining pleasure with the idea.

"Please, for me Autumn. I can tell you don't want to go, but this would be a great journey for both of us. A chance at a new life, a new opportunity. We can forget the awful past that keeps us held captive in this insane world. Please, I cannot do this without you." Autumn had started to form a slight grin.

"I don't want you to do this without me, so I'm in. But let me write a letter to my parents. They need to know that I love them still."

I smiled and said, "Okay! Great! Now you need to get your bag and we are leaving right now! But just one more thing, please do not write a letter. We cannot afford to waste time and drop it off"

"It will be fine," she responded. "I will just text them a letter and then turn off all traces of location trackers." I nodded in agreement.

Autumn guided me to her locker and we grabbed her backpack and other needed materials we found digging through her old and rusted locker. She then pulled out her phone and texted her mother and father. The ones who she would be saying goodbye to forever. What came next was a shock to me. She slammed her phone on the ground and we ran out of the unsecured building, right through those dull metal doors.

As soon as we walked out of the school I told Autumn my plan. My plan was to go from Mend Wood, Pennsylvania to New York City. Autumn nodded in agreement and I took out my map and guided the way.

*I breathed in the blue skies, and breathed out the gray. I stared up at the crumbling ceiling. Resting my palm against my rainbow body pillow, I turned to look at the door, and the knob was turning. Thunder came from his voice, and ricocheted into my memories, my mild dismal mind. "AUTUMN! A C, YOU GOT A C ON YOUR SPANISH TEST! AND THAT'S NOT ALL YOU WORTHLESS PILE OF CRAP, YOU ONLY GOT A B ON YOUR MATH TEST!" He never came at me.*

*He never laid a hand on me, but his words left temporary bruises until they had healed, and then it would start all over again. Unlike my best friend Melody, I never scarred from the attacks. I never got physically hurt.*

# Chapter 9

"We have to lay low," I said, "We cannot get caught out here, or else we won't have a chance to escape ever again."

"I agree," Autumn responded.

We could smell a vivid aroma of fresh baked blueberry pies and apple crisp as we trailed down, laying low, through our small and lonely town. It smelled absolutely delicious and scrumptious. We yearned so badly to just have a bite of it and dig into some crispy treats. But we had our minds set on a goal, a journey, one we had to accomplish and complete.

The streets of Mend Wood were small and filled with just air and no people whatsoever. That would make complete sense considering everyone was at work or at school at the time. The paved path felt smooth and cool to my feet that were covered with blue tennis shoes. The sweet smell of desserts was still vivid as ever. I looked across the street and said a mental goodbye. All of the little shops I once used to adore, all of the restaurants filled with mouth-watering treats, and the calm sense of home was all starting to disappear. It was all for a great cause. I needed this chance, this go on life. I just couldn't imagine what Autumn felt like. It was just now that I came to the realization that I basically forced my best friend to run away with me, not just to go with me, but to leave her friends, her family, and her home as well.

"I am so sorry Autumn. I guess I didn't realize what I was doing until now," I apologized.

"It's alright Melody. I understand. I am sad, yes. Disappointed? No! You need this, and I care about you so much Melody."

I felt my whole body shiver just at the words that had come out of Autumn's mouth. She was full of empathy, too much some people would say. But this was the first time that I truly felt like people cared about me and for me. Well, at least one person anyway: Autumn. She is giving up everything for a friendship with me. Nothing felt more special than that. And nothing could ever feel more momentous and special than that, ever.

We were reaching the very edge of town, the precipice to the end. Autumn and I looked at each other. "Ready?" she asked.

"More than ready," I said with a smile as we headed out of the border of Mend Wood.

# Chapter 10

Our feet ached in horrible pain. We had been walking for at least a few hours. I don't know, maybe two, three? I couldn't tell you what city we were in even if you gave me a map. I can't read a map to save my life. Because of this, Autumn and I decided to just wing it.

It was becoming cold as the day turned into evening, and evening turned into night. And it didn't help at all that it was October, and fall was beginning. It was becoming more chilly. I stopped and grabbed a sweatshirt and sweater out of my bulky backpack. "Here, put this on," I said to Autumn, handing her the baggy sweatshirt.

"Are you sure you will be warm enough with that sweater Melody?"

"Yeah, I will be warm enough. We can switch off every other day. It is the least I can do."

"Thanks Melody," Autumn responded.

"So, where should we spend the night?" I asked.

"Well, we are in country area now. I am sure we can find a shack, a shed, or a barn and we could lay our blankets down and sleep there?"

"That is perfect," I responded. "How about we keep going a little longer. Maybe an hour, and then after an hour, the minute we find a barn, shed, or shack, we will camp there."

The idea sounded perfect. My guess was that we would be in farmland almost all day tomorrow as well. The aroma of fresh grass became an unpleasant scent of cow poop and pig pens, if those even have a scent. The view of green grass also faded. Now all we saw was dirty and musty colored grass that had just the littlest tints of green hidden beneath the surface, barely lucid to the human eye.

The night air had felt cool and calming. I looked over across the field and saw a little red abandoned shack, or at least it looked abandoned or not in use.

"How about we sleep there tonight?" I suggested pointing to the shack.

"Good idea. I am beat, and I can't go on any longer." I nodded in agreement and we started heading towards the shed.

It took a bit to get there. Our pace had definitely slowed down, but by the time we got there, we were excited to see that the shack was in fact abandoned and unlocked. As soon as we entered the little shack, we heard a little chirp from the corner. It was pitch black inside, so I rummaged through the cumbersome backpack and dug around until I found the flashlight. Autumn grabbed the flashlight from me and turned it on, flashing the radiant light toward the corner of the shack. All of a sudden, a little baby yellow chick with a bright yellow beak and fluff coming from all sides of its adorable, petite little body came into view and trotted toward us.

"Well, would you look at that!" I exclaimed in a whisper, trying to not scare the baby chick away.

"It is a baby chick! Oh, how cute and adorable!" Autumn gasped.

"Oh no! It must have been shut up in here for a while with no food or water!" I exclaimed.

Autumn quickly tore through the backpack and ripped open a granola bar and started feeding bits and pieces to the little chick. In the meantime, I grabbed a bottle of water we had opened earlier and poured some into the cap, allowing the chick to quench his or her thirst after devouring bits of the crispy granola bar.

"We have to release it to the wild," Autumn said.

"I agree, I just wish we didn't have to see the cutie go!"

"Me too, but we have to do what is best for its survival, and if it is still outside the shack in the morning then we will feed it some more."

"Great idea," I said as I walked towards the chick to pick it up. The fur was a little dirty and crusty, but otherwise it was full of fluff and softness, and was extremely calming. It chirped some more as Autumn opened the door. We walked outside and made a nest for the chick out of shredded blades of grass.

"Good night little chick!" Autumn said as we entered the shack once again.

I could feel that the chick had released some endorphins in my brain, and my mood had become better at that moment. It had become calm and celebratory, elated I would say.

Despite the excitement of finding the little chick, it took no time for us to doze off and enter our dreams. Dreams of our new future that awaited. For the first time, I actually felt hope, felt like something was actually going to work out, and I couldn't have asked for a better companion to come along.

# Chapter 11

I felt like my mind had been hit by a huge, tragic, and disastrous hurricane. There was no hope. I just had great and tremendous sadness.

I opened my eyes and saw Autumn fast asleep in the midst of the cool, calm night. I, however, was awake, running a marathon with my own thoughts, listening to the crickets chirping and singing in the distance right outside the little red shack. The little red shack where two unearthly girls were trying to sleep, far away from where they used to call home.

Although everything was pitch black, my mind could picture the dark red siding of the shack and it blended perfectly with the agricultural aroma, chirping of crickets, and cool breeze that layered the outside of my warm cocoon of a blanket. I felt at peace finally. My mind had come back to reality and the part where I know I am safe and sound.

The whole feeling felt like the time when my father had left on a business trip…

*It was a cool and breezy night. The windows were lit up with precious moonlight. My mother lay with me on the brown fuzzy sofa and began singing to me as she cradled me, her 5-year-old daughter, in her arms. "Rockabye angel, sleep tight, calm your mind and drift to sleep, the ocean is here, waiting for you, sailing you across the sea." Her words seemed flawless. Her voice came from heaven and I felt truly safe, cradled in my own mother's arms, I was loved, and I was happy. I could hear her voice in unison with the chirping of crickets and all sorts of bugs as I drifted to sleep in her arms, where I truly knew she would be safe, and I would be too.*

I could remember those sweet words exactly. It was just her and me, and we were safe. Everything changed a few years after, oh how my life has changed because of that. Now I am just a 13-year old girl, face to face with the wild, and reality. But at least I could hear the stunning voice of my mother, and I could hear it as I drifted off into a beautiful slumber.

*The air had a vivid taste of fresh fruit and a scent of lovely green grass. The view of roses, daisies and tulips paralyzed my mind into an interminable view and vibe of safety and serenity. Of all the wonderful things the Earth has blessed us with, mother nature was by far the best and most rewarding. It could turn your worst days into a day full of peace and rejuvenation and supply the warmth of the summer breeze into a calm and relaxing mood. I heard a few thumps from the tall blades of grass across the field. A brown and white bunny hopped and trailed its way to me. It had the most adorable brown patch around its eye and had a smile like no other. It nibbled on my hand as I reached out to feed it a freshly grown orange carrot from a garden nearby. It was cheerful and loving, caring, and gentle. After devouring the carrot, it curled up near me and hinted to massage its soft fur. I curled my hands around the fluff of the bunny and let my hand sink deep into the fur, allowing the bunny to be calm and rested, and I felt happy. The bunny suddenly jumped away and sprinted into the blades of grass. I looked up and saw the dark gray clouds soaring and surrounding the once blue skies up above. The droplets of rain trickled on my nose and the thump struck everything around us. The once calm feeling had vanished into thin air, and lightning was attacking the nearby trees and flowers. Leaving me terrified, and sprinting to find shelter. My mind rushed from one thought to another. I cannot hide beneath a tree, or in the grass, or out in the open! I was trailing down the fields, and I kept running down the wet and soaked fields, through dead flowers, and fallen trees, staring up at the swirling winds up above. They were crawling closer, creeping towards me, and light struck me like an avalanche.*

"Melody, wake up! We have to get going if we want to reach New York state by nightfall tomorrow!" The light of the sun was lucid even through the small cracks of the shed. Autumn's voice startled me and awoke me from my dream. I emerged and stretched my arms out and felt sweat dripping from my forehead.

"Are you okay?" Autumn asked with concern.

"Yeah, I just had a nightmare," I responded. "How did you sleep?" I asked.

"Fine. You could say I slept like a rock."

"We better get our stuff packed and ready, and maybe feed that chick if it is still out there," I said folding my blanket into the backpack.

"Agreed," Autumn responded.

In less than five minutes, we were packed and headed for the journey of today. We stepped out of the shack and were utterly disappointed. The chick had wandered off during the night, heading on a journey of its own.

"Oh well," I said. "The chick will find some seeds to eat or something." We brushed it off our shoulders and headed toward the direction we had left off last night. Where was that again? Worry had entered all of my limbs once again and I became flushed with anxiety.

"I don't know what direction we came from," I said.

"Hey, calm down. If we look back to the shack, we could see the side of the door from where we were, so let's look," Autumn suggested, much braver than I was. My dream had freaked me out. How could something so calm and promising turn into something so exposed and vulnerable? I felt absolutely no peace at the moment. Nature usually gave me lots of calming vibes, but not today. It was not like that today at all. We looked back and the angle of the door was exactly where we hoped and prayed it would be. We were heading in the right direction. Now we just needed to continue our path north.

About an hour passed. Our thirst was growing strong, to the point where we had to stop because we couldn't go on any further. We sat down, the cool October air minimized the thirst tremendously. If it had been summer, we would be suffering fifty times worse. Because of our very limited supply of water, we decided to only drink half a bottle a day, so one bottle a day total. By the time we reached a nearby town, we would be out of water, so we would need to purchase some more. I hoped we could find one of those extremely cheap deals like three for ninety nine cents. I lunged and took my overly packed backpack off and rested it on the grass, which was much greener and fresher where we were now. I pulled a water bottle out of my bag and took a few gulps. Autumn then did the very same and we decided to take a rest for a bit to rejuvenate.

We sat in the dry and forbidding grass, breathed in the cool fall air, and watched the pretty fall-colored leaves of red, orange, yellow and brown fall gracefully to the ground.

"So, how are you liking our adventure?" I asked Autumn.

"It's alright, you know, we are making progress. Making progress to a happier lifestyle."

"Yeah," I responded.

"Did you talk to Mrs. Langer before we left?" Autumn asked with her gentle tone I just adored.

"Yeah, I walked into her office, I said thank you, and this is goodbye for a long time. I just left after that. Stormed out of her office. That is why we needed to leave so soon. She would have called me back down. Probably thought I was going to commit suicide or something."

"Yeah, well at least you got to say thank you. Could you tell me what happened at your group home last weekend?"

"Umm, what do you mean?" I asked with a sly amount of dumbness in my voice.

"Don't act stupid. I heard it all over the news. You should talk about it Melody. Talking has always helped me with my problems. It can inspire you to make the right decisions," Autumn responded.

"Are you saying that because I don't talk as much as I should, I am making the wrong decisions, like this one?" I responded with a sudden anger in my voice.

"In a way, yes. You cannot just abandon your problems. It doesn't work like that Melody. You need to talk through them and learn to cope with them."

"Then why did you come along Autumn? Is this just a joke? Are you playing me to think that you care about me?"

"I do," she responded, "I really do. I care about you very much. That is why I came along, because I knew nothing was going to stop you. I would never have let my very best friend run away alone. I could never lose you Melody. You mean the absolute world to me, and I adore you to pieces. I would worry about you constantly, every day, every night, every second. It would kill me to not know if you were safe, or even alive. That is why I came with you. We can turn this bad decision into one we won't regret."

That was one of the things I loved most about Autumn. She made so much sense. She always looked at the bright side of things, even when everything seemed bad. She always made me feel like home was wherever she was. She was my best friend, and I didn't want to lose her. I couldn't lose her. I wouldn't be able to bear the pain of it. She is all I have left. My best friend, my only friend, and my only family.

"Thanks, you are absolutely right Autumn. You are so amazing. Thank you for coming with me."

"You're welcome Melody," she responded in her kind and loving voice.

"We should probably get going," I suggested.

"Agreed. We have had plenty of time for physical and mental rejuvenation and rest. We arose from where our bottoms were planted and I pulled my backpack all the way to my shoulders, and we continued our journey once again.

We walked across rugged plains, dense grass, flat land, and hill top mountains, and we were still only in Pennsylvania. We were surely coming further. We were about one day away from reaching New York. Then it wouldn't be far until we would reach New York City from there.

Hours had passed with Autumn and I chatting about the adventures and fun we would have in New York City. We were talking about where we would sleep, eat and how to find a job for 13-year-olds. It couldn't be that hard. Homeless children find jobs every day. We could sleep in some stores, after closing hours of course, and then transfer until we would be able to find an abandoned building or something. It would be a place where we could call home, and call ours. It seemed like a very plausible plan. It would take a lot of effort, but we were completely up for that. We would need to go many more great lengths to accomplish our overall goal, but I had no doubt that would accomplish it, and have a life we had dreamed for.

We had given up everything, food, shelter, and even love in some areas. But, we gave it up so we could have so much more. We have to be entered into the reality and harshness of life eventually. Sure, 13 was a young age, but we were ready, and we were excited, nervous, and scared; but those are all emotions that life comes with. We have to learn to accommodate those feelings and push through, no matter how hard they might become. We would overcome this turmoil and despair and have hope. Today started out as a bad day, but at the end of it, as I lay here in the grass staring at the midnight moon and glistening stars, I see hope, and I see a future.

That night, I could picture my mom's body in the morgue. I hadn't seen her in there, but she had been there. She had been cremated, and was now in a grave. I missed her so. I missed her so much. I remember her hair, scent, and her beautiful eyes. But knowing that she was up in heaven, and that my father couldn't hurt her anymore, I was happy, and more comfortable with the fact that she was gone. Because she was safe, and that was how I was able to sleep through that night, where the celestial stars shone upon me.

## Chapter 12

I opened my eyes, sleepy and tired and looked over to see Autumn still resting on the park bench. The city lights had come on early and were flashing. Billboards of Hamilton caught my attention and so did the news reporter on the big screen that was platformed against several buildings in this great city. I looked up at the city clock that was just barely visible from through the subway railings. It was 6:00 a.m., bright and early. The town would be awakening soon and the city would become a huge tourist destination and the streets would be crowded and plentiful.

Autumn and I had made it here about 3:00 a.m. It was no surprise that she was still snoozing, and that I could barely keep my eyes open. The three day journey was long and tiring, and left us both exhausted. We made it here though, through all the fields, grass, storms, hills, ponds, and new city lights, we made it here to our destination: New York City, where we were planning to make our future and live a happy life.

We were thinking about enrolling ourselves in school—education had always been important to us—but we would have to use a fake name, not our real ones.

I was startled and interrupted in my thoughts when I heard Autumn stretch and awaken from her slumber. "Gosh, what time is it?" she asked.

"About five after six," I responded.

"Oh gosh, we barely got any sleep. What's the plan for today?" Autumn replied yawning.

"I think that we might walk around Central Park and check out the city. If you are alright with that?"

"Oh, definitely, as long as we can find a time to take a little cat nap in between all this," Autumn said.

"Yeah, doubt we will be able to find a quiet place in this busy city during the daytime," I said with laughter.

We packed up our things and started to head toward a nearby shop. The sign read *Anthony's Treasures*. Interesting, probably a thrift shop. We walked in and saw a beautiful array of golden lined walls and beautiful historical paintings and mantels. We looked around for a restroom and spotted several historical "treasures," beautiful and wonderful artifacts and thrift items. They were awfully expensive, however. There were lines of gorgeous dresses that looked like they came directly out of the Victorian Era. With lace trimming, maroon and blue colors, and old silk material, there was no doubt in our minds that these were authentic and true quality.

There was no bathroom in sight. I walked up to a nice gentlemen in a gold trimmed dress top and asked, "Excuse me sir, do you have any restrooms in here?"

"Yes we do ma'am, right over that way," he said with pleasure pointing to his left.

"Thank you," we paused for a moment and looked at his name tag, "Anthony."

He must have been the owner of this great and authentic shop.

The bathrooms looked like something that came out of the Titanic, beautiful and stunning. With a single golden toilet and sink, the beauty was way more admirable. The mirror was trimmed in radiant jewels and was shiny and neat. I didn't want to leave this place. It was so beautiful, like nothing I have ever seen before. Autumn and I quickly brushed our teeth and combed our hair with our fingers. I was sure to pack an extra toothbrush for Autumn before I left. But I was stupid and forgot to bring a hair brush and shampoo. Thankfully I brought deodorant because we haven't showered in days.

We were very hesitant to exit the beautiful restroom, but we did and quickly walked back to the line of dresses and decided to take another few looks at them.

"Interested in those dresses, yes?" We were startled when we heard the man's voice again.

"Yes, they look so authentic," Autumn replied. The man had appeared like he would have a British accent, looking at his attire, baby blue eyes and dark brown hair, but he had a casual, gentle, American accent.

"Yes, they are very authentic. My family and I have many ancestors who come from many parts of the world. We inherited many items from them. We are also big collectors of all things historical and unique. These dresses came from my great grandmother herself. She and her sisters wore these to some of their most extravagant balls back in the Victorian era," Anthony, the man said.

"They are very pricey," I said.

"Well, yes, they are. We price them high because of the historical value they hold, and just look at the quality."

"Do you do good business here? You must. Everything here is so beautiful and different," I said kindly.

"Yes, we make enough money to get by. This is just one of the businesses we own here in New York City. My wife, Celia, and I own an historical restaurant down the street, and we own a small regular kind of thrift store. I work full-time here, and my wife works full-time at the restaurant, along with employees we have hired for all of our businesses," Anthony responded.

"Wow that is great. You have really done something great with your life," Autumn said with weary in her voice.

"Yes, I am sure you two have great plans for your life as well. You will accomplish greatness."

"Well, we are only 13 and..."

"And we have a lot to plan yet," Autumn interrupted.

"That is right, you girls have plenty of time until you have to know what you need to do. Granted, Celia didn't know she wanted to be a cook and a business owner until she was 25. Well, are you lovely girls interested in buying anything? Did your parents give you money?"

"Umm..." I said, "Well, we don't really have parents right now..."

"Melody! I am so sorry sir, we have to go," Autumn said as she pulled me out of the store, yanking on my sore arms.

"What are you thinking!" she hollered at me as soon as the little bell rang signaling we exited the store. "You cannot just go telling a stranger everything!" she continued.

"I wasn't trying to expose us. Just maybe he could have helped us. He could have given us some food, water, or even money," I suggested.

"Well, you cannot just assume that someone will. What if he calls Child Protective Services! We would have been caught!"

"I guess I didn't think about that," I said looking over to the store window where I could see Anthony listening in on our conversation. "I am sorry okay? Let's just go and find a gas station or something, some place we can eat," I suggested.

Autumn nodded her head in agreement and sighed as we headed down the crowded sidewalks of New York City. As we were walking, we listened to the police sirens blaring past us—probably some car chase—watched the pigeons eat bread crumbs off the road and swoop down on a lady's shoulder, and took in the scents of hot dogs and pizza that were filling the air, igniting our taste buds. Our stomachs lurched in hunger.

The minute we found a gas station, we sprinted inside and had a shopping spree on yogurt and granola bars, using a quarter of my money. Thank goodness everything was on sale. We binged and binged on our treats and indulged in the sensation of being full and stuffed again. Today would be a long day, but we had to keep pushing through and venture throughout New York, hopefully finding an abandoned building somewhere. Surely there has to be one in this large city.

## Chapter 13

The comfort of the memory foam mattress supported my whole aching body. The soft and satin blankets covered my bare limbs and allowed me to rest in peace. I opened up my eyes and blinked once, staring at the little ray of sunlight creeping in through the shades. I stared out to the other side of the room. Autumn was sitting at the wooden desk, writing in her new journal where she would document her new life. The door was cracked open, just enough to hear Mr. and Mrs. Matthews down the hall preparing breakfast. The black dresser had four drawers open and empty, just waiting for belongings to be stuffed and left in there.

"Good morning Melody," Autumn whispered from across the new and calming room of white wallpaper, wooden trimming, and hardwood oak flooring.

"Good morning. Why are you whispering?" I asked in a whisper as well.

Autumn burst into laughter. "I am not quite sure," she said.

"Shall we head out and munch on some breakfast?" I suggested.

"Sure!" Autumn replied, pushing in the desk chair and heading toward the door.

The man, Mr. Matthews, had beautiful dark brown

hair that looked more like a black color. He had stunning and piercing blue eyes that shaped his whole form of his face. Mrs. Matthews wore a bright blue sleeved dress that matched wonderfully with her dirty blond hair and baby blue eyes. They were the perfect couple, and their names were Anthony and Celia.

*We were walking down the streets of New York City. The rays of the sun had become blinding to our sight. We heard a familiar voice down the road. The voice belonged only to Anthony from Anthony's Treasures, the historical thrift store we had come across the very first day we entered this great city. We hadn't expected to see him again, being that we tried to avoid his shop as much as possible after I spilled some of our personal story that could get us thrown all the way back to Mend Wood, Pennsylvania. We stopped in our tracks, frozen by worry and turned around to face Anthony.*

"Hey girls, I have been keeping my eyes peeled for you," he said in an actually kind manner. "I couldn't help but overhear a couple days ago when you two were talking about running away from your home I would assume. I will give you a chance to explain your story. I know there is always another side to it. If it seems reasonable, then I will not have to call Child Protective Services. Please, tell me your story first. I don't want to make the mistake of sending you back to a potentially dangerous living situation. I know how that can be." His voice was kind and well prepared. He must have been planning to talk to us for a while.

"Can you give us a second?" Autumn asked Anthony.

"Absolutely," he replied.

Autumn pulled me to the side near a park bench. "What if he is a predator?" Autumn asked.

`"Well, if he is, he wouldn't be approaching us in midday surrounded by several citizens and officers," I suggested.

"Well, you have a point there. Maybe we can tell him a little.

*It is worth a shot and the risk. Hopefully he won't call protective services," Autumn replied a little reluctantly.*

*"Okay, but let us only talk about how I am in a foster care group home and have no parents, and your parents have emotionally abused and neglected you. Even if that isn't the whole truth, it should be enough to support why we ran away from our city anyway."*

*"Okay, I agree," Autumn said.*

*We approached Anthony again. "We are ready," I said.*

*"Okay, would you girls like some coffee or a pastry? I can take you to a nearby cafe and we can talk there," he offered.*

*"Sure," I said thanking him.*

*We walked up to a big glowing sign that read, "Mandie Mini Café." We entered the building and took a seat at a three-person, marble countered table with three little silver chairs that surrounded the circular beauty. A lady came straight up to us and asked us what we would like to order.*

*"I will have a Salted Caramel frappe," I said.*

*"And I will have a chocolate turnover with whipped cream and chocolate sauce on the side," Autumn suggested.*

*"Lastly, I will have a Vanilla Bean Caramel frappe with extra caramel and macchiato," Anthony said with a kind thanks to the waitress as he handed her the menus.*

*"So, girls, do you want to start explaining your situation to me?"*

*"Yes," I started. "We ran away from our old city for many reasons. Umm, I was in a foster care system group home because I don't have any parents or living relatives."*

*"And I, had been emotionally abused and neglected by my parents, but I continued to live with them. Once Melody told me that she was running away, I couldn't let my best friend leave without me. I would be too worried about her," Autumn continued.*

*"Alright then. I thought you two were sisters, but you're best*

*friends. That is really sweet. What are your names?" Anthony asked.*

*"I am Melody, and this is Autumn," I said introducing ourselves.*

*"You girls have a tough situation. I don't think calling protective services will help with your issues, both emotionally and physically. I am going to offer you a place to stay. My family and I have an extra guest bedroom you two could share. It has a dresser, closet, desk, and two beds already inside of it. We can supply you with clothes and food, love if you want that. We have two children, Milo and Annie. They are both 12, around your age I would guess. If you want to stay with us, you are more than welcome. If you don't, we will have to call Child Protective Services."*

*Before we could respond, the waitress arrived with our order. "Thank you," we all said and continued our conversation.*

*Autumn and I looked directly at each other. We could read each other's minds it felt like. A grin formed ear to ear on our faces, and we nodded our heads.*

*"Great!" Anthony said. "You can call me Mr. Matthews, and you can call my wife Mrs. Matthews. For now, let's just enjoy this treat. After this, we can head to the house. Tomorrow, we will go shopping for some necessities, you know, hair brush, tooth brush, clothes, and whatever girl stuff you may need.*

## Chapter 14

We finally had a place to stay. A real and comfortable bed and the sweet smell of love that surrounded it. Anthony and Celia Matthews have been more than kind to us. They have given us everything we could ask for. They have even let us try on some of the stunning dresses from Anthony's!

We were sitting down at the marbled and speckled round table in the dining room of the condo we were staying in. Milo and Annie, the tweens here, sat right across from Autumn and I at the table. Sprawled out in front of us was a glorious stack of cinnamon French toast and maple syrup with a fruit bowl on the side. This reminded me purely of when I saw the scrumptious food over at the group home, but I knew this would be different. I had faith, real faith that this would work out.

"So, Autumn, Melody, where did you guys come from again?" the brown headed and blue eyed 12-year-old boy, Milo, asked.

"Umm," I started.

"That is a personal question honey," Mrs. Matthews responded in our defense.

"Oh no, it's fine. We came from Pennsylvania, Milo," Autumn replied, grinning at Milo.

"That's pretty cool guys, but if it were my choice, I would

have chosen to live in California. It is much better, and has more of a nice temperature." That voice had come from the dirty blond haired and petite 12-year-old girl, Annie, who sat adjacent to us. Her smile was glistening and her blue eyes were radiant, much more so than the others. She was truly unique. Autumn and I could see from the minute we laid eyes on her, she was full of potential. Although, she did have one flaw, sass. But what teenage girl doesn't? Autumn and I adored her either way.

"Annie! Please don't be so rude to our guests!"

"MOM! I am begging you! My name is Anneke, NOT Annie! Please! I am turning 13 in a month. Don't you think I deserve to be called what I want?"

Everyone was silent. Annie, well Anneke I suppose, was right. She was turning 13 and I agreed with her 100 percent. I also understand parents as loving as Celia and Anthony also wanting to keep their little girl, well, a little girl as long as possible.

"Not to step into your boundaries," I started, "but I do agree with Anneke. I understand you wanting to call her whatever you wish, as she is your child; but she is also a teenager now and deserves some independence and respect."

The table had remained silent for the rest of breakfast. After Autumn and I devoured the meal, we hurried to our room to finish organizing all of our stuff. Mr. Matthews had set this day for us to adapt and make accommodations to this new living situation. We would have the whole day to organize, get to know our new "roommates" and buy whatever materials we may need.

It really, truly was a miracle that Autumn and I were able to have met Anthony. If we hadn't, I can't imagine where we would be right now. In all honesty, our original plan was foolish. It was very foolish and filled with erroneous details. I could have seen us becoming more helpless and in even more despair. More danger, and more worry would have arisen from that as a result.

The day had passed rather quickly and dusk was arriving in a hurry, leaving celestial stars to carry our burdens away. Nights have become truly easier ever since Autumn and I were blessed with this home, and family. I was able to drift into a slumber, with peacefulness, and elated moods.

# Chapter 15

The forbidden night lay in the palms of a master. A master of all disguises. He, the one who had betrayed all. He was the one who had slammed his minivan into my grandparents' car all those years ago. He was the one wearing the mask, the one holding the real gun, and the one who didn't lay in a prison cell for murder.

My hope for the future was shattered just hours later when the blanket I was lying under was pulled out from under me and placed upon my head, suffocating me. I listened to night, the screams, of my own? I could not tell, but the screams of Autumn were vivid, vivid and true. My hair was being pulled and snarled by the hands of the gentleman I once thought him to be. My body was limp, my emotions numb. I couldn't fight, I couldn't breathe, I couldn't even reach my hand to meet Autumn's. It had all became a black and solemn night. I couldn't believe Mr. Matthews, the kind man who had welcomed us into his home, actually represented true evil.

My eyes were fluttering, my vision blurry. I could smell rotten pipes and feel the forbidden cement. I felt violently bare, and significantly in despair. Clearing my eye sight, I looked over to my right, and Autumn lay passed out to my side. Her hair in strands, and bruised as can be, tears flooded down my eyes. This was all my fault. I had led my best friend into this crazy idea of peace and happiness, and now she lay here beside me, suffering with agony. And it was all because of me. He had betrayed me, betrayed us. He had lied. He was a coward! He crept through the night and kidnapped us, captured us, and put us into this rotting room, this cold and bare room, to die. There was no food, no water, no happiness. What about Anneke and Milo? Was this all a play? Did they fool Autumn and I? I couldn't believe it, this devious family, this horrendous family, this family of lies and sins. Now, I lay here, staring up at the ceiling. I can almost hear the steps and clunks of people awaking and arising upstairs. We must be in the basement of Mr. and Mrs. Matthews' house, if that even is their real names.

I had to wake up Autumn. We had to find a way out of here. There was no way I would be able to stand living in this freezing cold and bare basement without any food or water, and I doubt Mr. and Mrs. Matthews would help us out. We were doomed, it was our fate. I crawled over to where Autumn was resting silently. I haven't heard a peep from her all morning, not even a breath of air. My worry was escalating. She had to be alive. I couldn't live without her. I placed my hand on her shoulder. She and I were both covered in brown rags, old and musty, like dirty laundry. She didn't even shiver. She didn't even flinch.

"Autumn?" I whispered. No response, just her closed eyelids, her bare body, and bruises around her neck.

I couldn't control myself. My panic was rising, my breathing was stopping, my hair in my face, tears everywhere. I could feel myself fading away. I could feel her presence, but it wasn't actually here. I could feel her soul, but she was gone. All because of me. She had been strangled, and now she wasn't waking up. I dragged my friend along with me and she got killed because of it. She got killed for being the sweetest person on Earth, the most kind and generous soul. And now she was gone.

My face was buried within my knees. My whole body was shivering. I was shaking uncontrollably. My mind was nowhere and everywhere at the same time. I saw specks of red, specks of Autumn, specks of my mother, and specks of fate.

## Chapter 16

Warmth surrounded me. I felt like sunlight was radiantly shining through. The warm arms were curled around me, strangling me almost. I was in the basement, but the once freezing cement felt like soft carpet. The bitter cold had turned into warmth. I could feel it, the warm hands curling around me. The soul of my father. I could feel it deeply. It was my father who was holding me with his heart.

"Dear, dear. Don't be afraid honey."

I looked up. I saw the piercing blue eyes. I saw his lips, his hair. It was him. I knew it, I really knew it now.

"Dad, is that you?"

"Yes, my sweet Melody."

"You're my real dad…" I knew it. I knew it with all my heart. The moment I saw him in the treasury shop, the moment I laid eyes on him. My dad was here, my real dad. But my stepdad was in prison. In prison for a crime he never committed.

My real father, Mr. Matthews, had framed my stepdad for the murder of my mother. He had kidnapped me and Autumn, and trapped me in this basement. Now, he was here, acting like a real father, but it wouldn't last.

Fear struck me. Realization struck me again. I saw him, looked into his eyes. I saw the evil. I saw the temper. He was my birth father, yes, but not my dad! A dad is loving and kind, not like him, not like Anthony.

"YOU are the one who murdered my mother!" I exclaimed. I trampled out his arms. As I was reaching for the top of the staircase, I felt a slip of paper, a note maybe, slide into my hand. Ignoring it, I sprinted up the stairs, trotted through the house, and right out of that door, out of that condo, and out of Mr. and Mrs. Matthews' house. The door still remained frayed open behind me. I kept running. I turned my head once, and there he was. No, he was not chasing me, but instead he stood at the door, holding Autumn's bare, limp and dead body in his arms with a smirk plastered on his face.

# Chapter 17

I quickly trailed past the fleet of cars, down the valley of roads. I stared back at the blaring sirens of police cars heading towards the house. I couldn't stop now. I couldn't hold in the pain, I couldn't hold back the tears. My friend was really dead. My mother was really dead. My stepfather was really in jail for a crime he didn't commit, and my real father murdered the two most important people to me. I was left without anyone, without a hand to hold, or a friend to give me the warmth and respect I needed, the love I craved.

Just a few blocks away but within sight, I could see the beautiful waves crashing behind and over a bridge, a steep one indeed. The day was beautiful, and the paved road on the bridge was clear. The whole city felt empty. I felt at peace, at true peace.

I continued running down the road towards the glaring bridge that was in view. Then all of a sudden I remembered the note that was slipped into my palm all those minutes ago. I sat down on a blue park bench near the bridge, and gently unfolded the crinkled and damp piece of paper, and began reading…

*Melody, my dear child. I for one should apologize*
*right off the bat for not finding you sooner, for not*
*ending your mother's life sooner, and for not sending*

*that horrid stepfather of yours to jail before he got the chance to harm you and scar you with those hurtful words of criticism and painful bruises. Maybe you have pieced together already how I caused the death of your grandparents. What you don't know Melody is that not too long after, I threatened your stepfather with the promise that I planned to murder his loving wife, your mother. So, you're welcome sweetie, but it's too bad that your friend is off to heaven now isn't it?*

Now my mom lies in a grave, murdered by my real father, and my stepfather grieves in prison, framed for a murder he didn't commit. My best friend lies probably in a morgue by now, and here I am leaning over a bridge railing, left with no other choice.

I was at the precipice of death. I leaned over the edge and took in the scent of the river breeze and listened to the excruciating thunder of the waves that were interminable. There were seconds before I would launch myself into those threatening waters far below and execute myself once and for all. I knew that all of the pain and misery would finally be terminated. I closed my eyes... and took a leap, aiming at the threatening waters.

# Chapter 18

I felt a solemn yank hurdle my arm inwards, away from the crashing waters. I felt the tears sliding down my cheeks, making a river of their own. My vision was blurry, my breathing rapid. I felt the palms of a lady pull me to the ground, off the landing and onto the concrete path. Her hair was pulled back in a perfect bun, and to my surprise it was Mrs. Langer who had saved me, who had pulled me away from guaranteed death. I could feel the breeze slather against my cheeks, drying my tears, as I looked at Mrs. Langer's calm smile, looking straight at me.

"Thank you," I whispered as Mrs. Langer held me in her arms.

"Hush now dear, it will be alright. I promise. Honey, you have so much more to live for. You are a beautiful and amazing human being, and you can't control others' actions, even as they affect you. The only person you can control is yourself." Her voice was calm and smooth.

I heard the sirens nearby. The ambulance pulled up hurriedly and came to a sudden halt near the bridge. Mrs. Langer gently released me and walked with the greatest of ease up to one paramedic, handing him a note written by me, as another paramedic, a short, black-haired woman in her mid-thirties came to me and wrapped me in an American Red Cross blanket.

*Goodbye to everyone I had loved, everyone who is gone. Goodbye to those still alive, Mrs. Langer, Amber Lee, and Liberty. And greetings to whom I shall meet in heaven, Caitlyn, Autumn, Mommy, and other victims of this cruel world.*

*Love, Melody Potter.*

It is true. I had written a suicide note, and attempted to jump off a bridge and kill myself, but I was saved. I was saved by just one of many people who loved and cared for me. This wasn't the end of my story. I don't see an end in the near future, for I will keep persevering and never lose my chance to have a family and real hope.

# What You Should Do

This novel showcases some real life struggles my fictional characters had faced. My purpose in telling this story is to show how people's actions and words can affect others. If Melody's real father had never murdered Melody's grandparents, and threatened her stepfather, then her life could have been dramatically different. This is the fictional story of innocent, yet clueless girls who made some careless choices in their lives, driven by mental illness, depression and anxiety.

**Living Situation/Homelessness:** If you are ever in an uncomfortable living situation as my character Melody was, or know someone who is, I would advise you to reach out to your school social worker, if you have one, or your school counselor. They can help get you the resources you need.

**Abuse:** If you or someone you know is suffering from any abuse or has gone through abuse, I encourage you to reach out to a trustworthy adult or school counselor. If it is a serious emergency, pick up the phone and dial 9-1-1.

**Suicide:** If you or someone you know is considering or has shown warning signs of possibly being suicidal, REACH out immediately to a school counselor, teacher, parent or guardian, or any trusted adult. It can make all the difference. If someone you know is in immediate danger to themselves or anyone else contact 9-1-1 immediately.

# Author's Note

Hello, I am Kayla Jarppi, author of *Heaven's Note*. The main reason I wrote this novel was to spread awareness about common mental illnesses, such as depression and anxiety. In this book, the main character has both and you get a feel for what it is like to be in her shoes and what her struggles are like. I tried to show how different life issues affect people day to day, and how much more they can affect people who are struggling with a mental illness.

Some of you may be asking why I chose the topic of depression and anxiety to base my story on. Well, the truth of the matter is that I struggle with depression and anxiety every day, and not enough people get the feel for how it really affects those who live with it.

My battle with depression started when I was 11-years-old. I did not realize what it was at first. I just felt so empty and lost in this big world. It was my first year at Hudson Middle School.

I tried to act like I was happy and be cheerful, but I didn't feel that way. Just the year before, my dad had moved out and my parents divorced. I deeply missed my dad. I was only able to see him on weekends at first, then he moved to Hudson. That is when I was able to see him every other week. It was a miracle for me, I was so happy.

My 6th grade year was going okay at first, but by the middle of the year everything turned upside down. A couple of boys in my advisory class started teasing me, yelling at me, and calling me stupid and awful. They said, "You'll never be anything. You're a nobody." I felt so empty inside. I would cry into my palms every single day in advisory. I felt like everything had come crumbling down. I felt like my happiness had burst into flames and turned into ash with no warning. I didn't know what to do. It continued on and on for a month or two.

Then it came to a sudden halt. They acted like everything was fine, like it was all good. They didn't name call or bully me. It was getting better, I thought. Then one day, a boy was "play" beating up another boy in advisory next to my desk. All of a sudden, the boy who was being "beat up" shouted, "Kayla stop hurting me! Ow! Kayla that hurt! Stop!" It was in the most fake voice I had ever heard.

Barely anyone stuck up for me that day, and the bullying started again. They were yelling and replaying the same words over and over again whenever they saw me, in classrooms, in the hallways. None of my teachers really did anything about this, and that hurt. The crying started yet again, and depression took over yet again. I felt hopeless. Like the other bullying, it ended eventually and the year was over.

The next year came so quickly. I was going into the 7th grade and was prepared for a good year. My depression had lingered throughout the summer, but wasn't as major. Seventh grade seemed awesome at first, until November. My depression escalated and anxiety officially started, and continued to escalate. That is when I started to write poetry. It was a coping skill that worked for a while. Since then I have written over 150 poems. That March is when my depression got even worse. I felt like I was at my breaking point. I couldn't take it anymore. It was a struggle to wake up every day, go to school, and deal with people, panic attacks, depression, and anxiety. That is when I reached out to my school counselor.

She has helped me through all of my struggles. She is one of the only people I can trust, and talk to honestly. I wouldn't be where I am right now, in recovery, without her and my other supports. She and my dad and teachers have been the best things that have ever happened to me because they promoted my recovery, and they support me. I am still in recovery, but it will get better and I never want to lose hope.

In my book, Melody doesn't reach out for real support, and I also wanted to spread awareness about that as well. Reaching out is key in recovery. I didn't reach out until about three months after my depression and anxiety started to get worse, and if I didn't reach out, things would have been a lot different.

At the end of my book, Melody attempts suicide because she couldn't bear the pain of life, but she was saved by her old school counselor, just one of many peole who care about her in the book. I want you to try to think of a different ending to the story that could have come about if she had reached out to her school counselor originally, before she ran off. My guess is that Melody would have found the resources like I did to cope and learn to manage.

The whole goal of this story is for you, the reader, to see the dangers people who live with mental illnesses face. Indeed, this was a very dramatic, and tragic story, but also something that could actually happen in real life. My message for you right now is to always know how special and unique you are, how much potential is inside of you, and all the talents that you have. Begin to utilize them today and never be afraid to SHINE!

# SIGMA'S BOOKSHELF

Sigma's Bookshelf (www.SigmasBookshelf.com) is an independent book publishing company that exclusively publishes the work of teenage authors, who are between the ages of 13 - 19. The company was founded in 2016 by Minnesota teenager Justin M. Anderson, whose first book, *Saving Stripes: A Kitty's Story*, was published when he was 14, and has since sold hundreds of copies.

"I know there are a lot of other teenagers out there who are good writers and deserve to have their work published, but don't have access to the kinds of resources I do. I wanted to help them," he said.

*Sigma's Bookshelf is a sponsored project of Springboard for the Arts, a nonprofit arts service organization. Contributions on behalf of Sigma's Bookshelf may be made payable to Springboard for the Arts and are tax deductible to the extent permitted by law. Donations can be made online at www.SigmasBookshelf.com/donate, and will help cover the expenses associated with bringing teenagers' books to market at no cost to them.*

www.ingramcontent.com/pod-product-compliance
Lightning Source LLC
Chambersburg PA
CBHW031953130726
47905CB00003BA/908